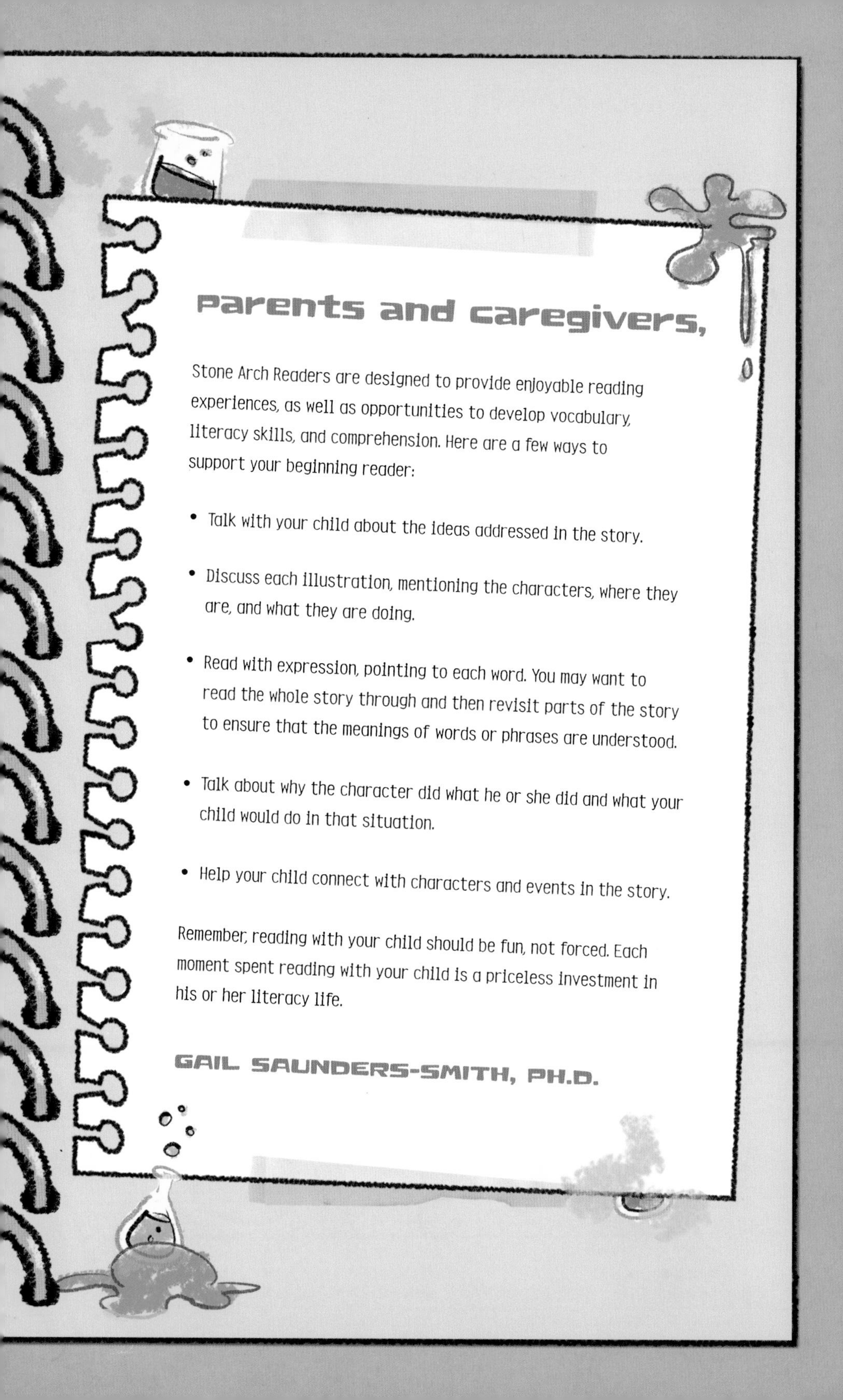

Parents and caregivers,

Stone Arch Readers are designed to provide enjoyable reading experiences, as well as opportunities to develop vocabulary, literacy skills, and comprehension. Here are a few ways to support your beginning reader:

- Talk with your child about the ideas addressed in the story.
- Discuss each illustration, mentioning the characters, where they are, and what they are doing.
- Read with expression, pointing to each word. You may want to read the whole story through and then revisit parts of the story to ensure that the meanings of words or phrases are understood.
- Talk about why the character did what he or she did and what your child would do in that situation.
- Help your child connect with characters and events in the story.

Remember, reading with your child should be fun, not forced. Each moment spent reading with your child is a priceless investment in his or her literacy life.

GAIL SAUNDERS-SMITH, PH.D.

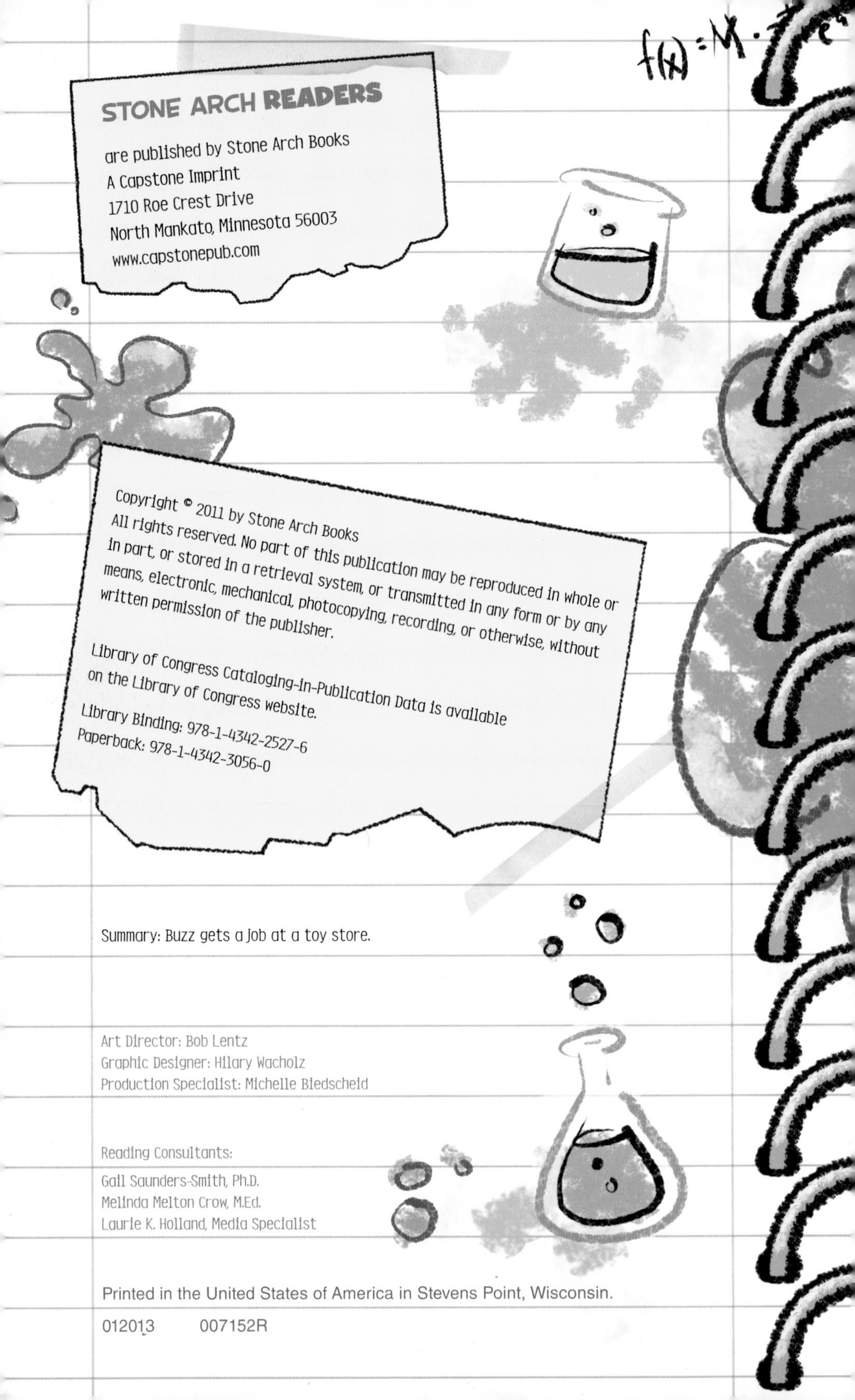

STONE ARCH **READERS**

are published by Stone Arch Books
A Capstone Imprint
1710 Roe Crest Drive
North Mankato, Minnesota 56003
www.capstonepub.com

Library of Congress Cataloging-in-Publication Data is available on the Library of Congress website.

Library Binding: 978-1-4342-2527-6
Paperback: 978-1-4342-3056-0

Summary: Buzz gets a job at a toy store.

Art Director: Bob Lentz
Graphic Designer: Hilary Wacholz
Production Specialist: Michelle Biedscheid

Reading Consultants:
Gail Saunders-Smith, Ph.D.
Melinda Melton Crow, M.Ed.
Laurie K. Holland, Media Specialist

Printed in the United States of America in Stevens Point, Wisconsin.

012013 007152R

BUZZ BEAKER AND THE GROWING GOO
Written by CARI MEISTER
Illustrated by BILL McGUIRE
STONE ARCH BOOKS
a capstone imprint

Buzz Beaker loves to make cool new stuff. He keeps his ideas in a special notebook.

The toy store owner needs to sell more science kits. Maybe Buzz can help.

GOO!
CH2
CH2
C=C
H
CH3
B
f(x)=(1-e^(-2/x))^b
A
CH3
O=C
O
C
H2
C
H
n
*

Buzz Beaker loved the toy store. He loved the castles.

He loved the magic sets and the train sets.

Most of all, Buzz loved the science kits.

The toy store had lots of science kits. They had human body kits.

They had weather kits.

They even had robot kits.

They were all wonderful.

Buzz spent a lot of time at the toy store. One day, the owner of the store talked to Buzz.

"Buzz, would you like a job?" she asked.

Buzz could not believe his luck. Of course he would like a job!

"Perhaps you can help me sell more science kits," the owner said. "They do not sell very well."

The next day, Buzz went to work at the store. The owner said, “Set up the kits in a way that will make people want to buy them.”

So Buzz did.

People liked the way Buzz set up the science kits. They asked Buzz questions about the kits.

But Buzz did not sell one kit. The shoppers bought games and trains instead.

Buzz tried something new. He juggled five kits. Everyone was surprised. People clapped.

But Buzz did not sell one kit. The shoppers bought dolls and balls instead.

That night Buzz brushed his teeth a long time. It helped him think.

"I know what to do!" he told his dog, Raggs. "Tomorrow, I will do a science show. Then people will see how cool the kits are."

The next day, Buzz told the owner his idea.

"Great!" she said. "Pick something you think will be popular."

Buzz looked at all the kits. Which one should he try?

Should he choose magnets or mummies?

Should he choose lightbulbs or rockets? It was hard to decide.

Then Buzz saw a box that read, "Fun with Goo."

"Perfect!" he said. "Everyone likes goo."

Buzz set up a table. He opened the goo kit.

He mixed.

He stirred.

It was ready!

The goo was sticky. The goo was slimy. It even glowed.

"The goo is cool," thought Buzz, "but there is only a little bit."

He dug in his backpack. He took out a small bottle. It was his dad's special potion. The potion made things bigger.

Buzz added a few drops to the goo. It worked! Soon everybody in the store looked at the goo.

They could not miss it. Goo was everywhere!

The store sold out of goo kits in a few minutes.

Soon Buzz had a new problem. The goo did not stop growing.

It kept growing and growing. Goo was taking over the store!

"Make it stop!" yelled the owner.

Buzz said some magic words. "Goo be gone!"

And it was!

That day all the magic sets sold out, too.

THE END

STORY WORDS

castles
science
human
wonderful
popular
magnets
potion

Total Word Count: 453

LOOK WHAT BUZZ IS BUILDING!